~ FREE ACCESSORIES ~

A SUPER BARGAIN!

FLYWEIGHT MUSCLEMAN

A lump of muscles!

NEVER EAT NASTY FOOD AGAIN!

Makes delicious pancakes

MAKE OTHER KIDS JEALOUS

The coolest model!

$175

Lucas

5' 7" – 154 lb. – Age: 35

$200

Olaf

5' 1" – 220 lb. – Age: 32

$325

Hal

6' – 176 lb. – Age: 26

NO LONGER PROPERTY OF

John

READS TO YOU EVERY DAY!

 TRADE-IN SPECIAL

Exchange your old model for a new one for free!

100% HIP

SPECIAL OFFER!

D0576074

OPEN 24 HOURS A DAY

For my dad

First published in Belgium and Holland by Clavis Uitgeverij, Hasselt – Amsterdam, 2015
Copyright © 2015, Clavis Uitgeverij

English translation from the Dutch by Clavis Publishing Inc. New York
Copyright © 2016 for the English language edition: Clavis Publishing Inc. New York

Visit us on the web at www.clavisbooks.com

No part of this publication may be reproduced or stored in a retrieval system, or transmitted in any form or by any means, electronic, mechanical, photocopying, recording, or otherwise, without the prior written permission of the publisher, except in the case of brief quotations embodied in critical articles and reviews.
For information regarding permissions, write to Clavis Publishing, info-US@clavisbooks.com

The Daddy Store written and illustrated by Sanne Miltenburg
Original title: *De papawinkel*
Translated from the Dutch by Clavis Publishing

ISBN 978-1-60537-266-2

This book was printed in October 2015 at Graspo CZ, a.s.,
Pod Šternberkem 324, 76302 Zlín, Czech Republic

First Edition
10 9 8 7 6 5 4 3 2 1

Clavis Publishing supports the First Amendment and celebrates the right to read

The Daddy Store

Sanne Miltenburg

Clavis

NEW YORK

We got a flyer for the Daddy Store in our mailbox today.
There are all sorts of dads in the Daddy Store.
Kind dads, tall dads, tough dads, funny dads....
I myself already have a dad. But he is dumb. When I jump
from the highest diving board into the swimming pool,
he doesn't even notice. And at the fair,
he thinks everything is too expensive.

I've had enough.
I am going to exchange my dad for a different one.

We are going into town.
"Come on, Dad," I say cheerfully.
"I am going to exchange you at the Daddy Store."
Dad looks a bit sad.

CHOOSE
YOUR COLOR

CHOOSE
YOUR TYPE

CHOOSE
YOUR SIZE

TRADE IN
YOUR OLD
MODEL FOR
A NEW ONE

RETURNS

The saleswoman gives me a friendly smile.
"This is a really fine example," she says.
"You can trade in your old dad for a new one.
Did you see our special offers?"
She points to a few dads behind glass.
They all look nice! After some thought,
I choose my new dad.

"Let's go for a swim!" I say to my new dad.
"What a wonderful idea!" he replies.
He stands at the side of the pool and watches me.
He nods proudly and calls out, "Have you seen him?
My fantastic son? Look at how fast he goes!"

When I jump from the highest diving board, my new dad
claps his hands so loudly that everyone stares at us.
I am so embarrassed, I duck under the water.
"You're so talented!" my new dad calls.
"You'll go to the Olympics next year!"
The pool attendant says he's yelling too loud
and makes him leave.

I sigh.
This dad is no good.
I'll have to exchange him for a different one.

In the Daddy Store, I choose a dad
who's already jumping up and down.
He has a ball in his hands.
"Let's go play soccer in the park!" he cries.
We decide to have a competition.
My new dad wins easily.

I try to kick the ball,
but he pushes me out of the way
and makes all the goals himself.
It starts to get dark in the park,
but he doesn't want to stop.
"Come on, you wimp!" he yells. "Just a few more games!"
"Can't... we... take a break?" I pant.
"Stop whining! Come on! Fifty more goals!"

I sigh. This dad is no good either.
I'll have to exchange him for a different one.

In the Daddy Store,
I choose a dad who looks cool.
"I'm a famous movie star," he says.
"Shall we go to the fun fair?"
I think that's a wonderful idea!
We drive there in his sports car.

At the fair, he tells me I can do whatever I want.
My new dad fills my pockets with money.
"You can go on as many rides as you want!" he says.
"Will you come with me?" I ask.
He shakes his head. "No, I am going to sign autographs."
The fun fair is no fun alone.

I sigh. This dad is no good either.
I'll have to exchange him for a different one.

At the Daddy Store,
a girl is looking at my dad.
"I want this one," she says.
"I was here first!" a boy calls.
"No, me!"
They get into a fight.
I run toward them.
"You shouldn't pick this one!"
I say loudly.

"Why not?"
"I just brought him back. He's very boring."
"Oh, well. Whatever!" the boy mumbles.
He and the girl walk away.

I hand in my ticket at the cashier's desk.
"**I want my old dad back,**" I say.
"Are you sure?" the saleswoman asks.
"**Yes!**"

At home, Dad and I order pizza,
and we watch my favorite movie. It's great.
We laugh at the same jokes and wrestle on the couch.
I give Dad a big hug.

You are the best dad in the world!

A store in every neighborhood!

The Daddy Store

Shop for your perfect dad!

Not good enough? Get a refund!

FATHER'S DAY SPECIAL
Every day an exciting new offer!

All kinds available!

New prototypes

NO LONGER PROPERTY OF PPLD

Alex

Ralph

Joe

Martin

ALL SIZES. ALL TYPES.